The Dancing Fairy

Did you know that all fairies have to go to school to learn how to be fairies? Well they do! They have to learn how to fly, how to be graceful and how to do magic. Some fairies find it difficult. Clementine did!

Poor Clementine. She was the worst in the class. She was clumsy and awkward. When they were dancing she was the only fairy who tripped over her own feet.

"Clementine! Think of feathers, not elephants," Madame Bouquet, the fairy dance teacher, was forever saying.

At the end of term all the fairies were given a

special task for the holidays. Sweetpea and Beatrice had to make garlands of flowers for the May Ball. Jemima and Poppy had to collect honey from the bees. Breeze and Scarlet had to polish the leaves on the holly tree.

But there was one task that no one wanted. This was to help a little girl who had measles.

"Clementine," said Madame Bouquet, "I want you to take this rose petal lotion, and paint it on the little girl's spots when she is asleep," said Madame Bouquet. "If you do this every night, for one whole week, the spots will disappear."

Clementine couldn't wait to start. That night she flew to the little girl's house and in through the bedroom window. So far so good! The little girl's name was Alice, and Clementine could see her fast asleep in bed. She was holding a fat, round teddy in her arms.

4

My Book of
Fairy
Stories

p

Contents

Clementine crept towards the bed. Then she tripped over the rug and sat on a prickly hairbrush which was lying on the floor.

"Ouch!" she yelled.

Alice stirred, but didn't wake. Clementine got up quietly. She bent over to pick up the hairbrush, and a toy clown, with a silly face, pinched her bottom!

"Ouch!" she yelled again.

This time Alice did wake up. "Who's there?" she asked sleepily.

"It's Clementine," said the fairy, "and your clown just pinched my bottom!"

"Never did!" said the clown.

"Are you sure?" Alice asked Clementine, rubbing her eyes. "He's usually very well behaved."

Then Clementine overbalanced and sat down quickly on Alice's hot-water bottle which was lying on the floor. It was so bouncy that she shot straight up in the air and landed with a plop on Alice's bed.

"Are you alright?" asked Alice, rubbing her eyes again, to make sure she wasn't seeing things.

Clementine smoothed her crumpled dress and fluttered her wings. She explained to Alice why she had come.

"I'm sorry I woke you," she added. "You're not really supposed to see me."

Alice didn't mind. She thought it was lovely to be able to talk to a real fairy.

"Can you really do magic?" she asked Clementine.

6

"Yes," Clementine told her. "I'm quite good at magic. I just wish I wasn't so clumsy."

She told Alice about her dance classes and Alice told Clementine about her ballet lessons.

"If you are helping me get rid of my measles," she said to Clementine, "I'll help you with your ballet."

So each night Clementine went to see Alice. Alice taught Clementine how to point her toes, how to keep her balance on one foot and how to curtsy gracefully. Clementine worked hard to copy everything Alice showed her. But it was the pirouette that Clementine did best of all. Holding her arms high above her head she twirled and twirled round Alice's bedroom.

In return, Clementine painted Alice's spots. Each

day they became fainter and fainter. By the end of the week they had gone.

After the holidays the fairies went back to school.

"Now fairies," said Madame Bouquet, "I want you to show me The Dance of the Sugar Plum Fairy."

The music started and the fairies began to dance. And, do you know, Clementine was the best dancer in the class. Madame Bouquet couldn't believe her eyes.

"Why, Clementine," she gasped, "you're my prima ballerina!"

And 'prima', as I'm sure you know, means 'first and best'!

Clementine was the happiest fairy in the world!

Sugarplum
and the
Butterfly

"Sugarplum," said the Fairy Queen, "I've got a very important job for you to do."

Sugarplum was always given the most important work. The Fairy Queen said it was because she was the kindest and most helpful of all the fairies.

"I want you to make a rose-
petal ball gown for my
birthday ball next week."

"It will be my
pleasure," said Sugarplum
happily. She liked being
busy.

She set to work straight
away. Sugarplum began to
gather cobwebs to make the
thread, and rose petals to make the dress. While she
was collecting the thread she found
a butterfly caught in a cobweb.

"Oh, you poor thing,"
sighed Sugarplum. She
stopped what she was doing
to help him. Very carefully,
Sugarplum untangled the
butterfly. But his wing was
broken. Sugarplum laid the
butterfly on a bed of feathers.

10

He was very sick and weak with hunger. Sugarplum gathered some nectar from a special flower and fed him a drop at a time. Then she set about mending his wing with a magic spell. Every day Sugarplum fed the butterfly with nectar and cast her spell to mend his wing. After six days, the butterfly was better. He was very grateful. But by now Sugarplum was behind with her work!

"I shall never finish the Fairy Queen's ball gown by tomorrow," she cried. "Whatever shall I do?" The butterfly comforted her.

11

"Don't worry, Sugarplum," he said. "We will help you." He gathered all his friends together. There were yellow butterflies, blue butterflies, red and brown butterflies. He told them how Sugarplum had rescued him from the cobweb and helped to mend his wing. The butterflies gladly gathered up lots of rose petals and dropped them next to Sugarplum. Then the butterflies flew away to gather more cobwebs, while Sugarplum arranged all the petals.

Back and forth went Sugarplum's hand with her needle and thread making the finest cobweb stitches. Sugarplum added satin ribbons and bows. When she had finished, Sugarplum was very pleased.

"Dear friend," she said to the butterfly, "I couldn't have finished the dress without your help."

"And I couldn't have flown again without your kindness," said the butterfly.

The Fairy Queen was delighted with her new ball gown. And, when she heard the butterfly's story, she wrote a special 'Thank You' poem for Sugarplum:

Sugarplum is helpful,
Sugarplum is kind.
Sugarplum works hard all day,
But she doesn't mind.
She always does her very best,
To make sick creatures well.
She brings such joy and pleasure
As she weaves her magic spell!

The Football Fairy

Georgina loved to play football. But there was just one problem.

"I'm fed up with these silly wings," she said, wiggling her shoulders. "They just get in the way."

The other fairies didn't agree at all.

"Whoever heard of a fairy without wings?" laughed Twinkletoes, doing a little dance.

"You wouldn't be able to fly if you didn't have wings," said Petal, landing on a flower.

"Flying is brilliant," called Sparkle, sprinkling fairy dust.

"Keep that fairy dust away from me," sneezed Georgina crossly. "I'm going to play football."

"Football is a game for elves, not fairies!" said Sparkle.

"In that case, I don't want to be a fairy!" said Georgina, and stamped off.

"She'll change her mind," said the wise fairy, "just wait and see."

But Georgina wouldn't change her mind. She pulled on her football boots and went to play with the elves.

The football game was very rough. The ball bounced around the field and, quite often, off the field! Sometimes it went up into the trees. Two birds who were trying to build their nest got very fed up, especially when the football landed near them.

Georgina flew up to get it. "Perhaps my wings can be useful after all," she

thought, landing on the ground. She looked round quickly, hoping no one had seen her.

But someone had! Barry, the elf, was a tell-tale! He couldn't wait to tell the fairies what he had seen.

"Ah," nodded the wise fairy. "I knew she would use her wings sooner or later." But Georgina still

17

wouldn't join in with the other fairies.

The next time she played football, the game was rougher than ever. One elf kicked the ball so hard it flew into the tree and hit the birds' nest. This time there was an egg in it! The egg began to topple.

None of the elves noticed; they were far too busy arguing with the referee. So Georgina flew up and, just in time, caught the egg before it hit the ground. Then she flew up to the nest.

"Thank you," said the mummy bird, rather sternly,

18

tucking the egg back under her. "But please, in future, be more careful when you play football!"

Georgina promised she would.

When she flew down from the tree, Barry the tell-tale elf saw her. Of course, he told the fairies. They looked knowingly towards Georgina. "What did I tell you?" said the wise fairy. "She'll soon come round to being one of us."

Next time she played football, Georgina checked the tree first. The mummy bird was away. "Good!" she thought. "She can't complain this time." But, thanks to a naughty elf, the football knocked into the birds' nest. A small bundle of feathers tumbled out. It was a baby bird!

Georgina spotted it and, quick as lightning, she flew up to catch him. Gently, she held him in her arms and flew back to the nest. When he was safely inside she sprinkled him with fairy dust to keep him from further harm. Just then mummy bird came back.

"I shall tell everyone about your kindness," she said, as her baby snuggled under her feathers. "And, as you're such a good fairy, will you be baby Beak's godmother?"

"I'd be delighted!" said Georgina.

When they heard the news, the other fairies were very proud of her.

"Perhaps it's not so bad being a fairy after all," grinned Georgina.

The Tooth Fairy

Pansy was nearly five. She couldn't wait for her birthday because Mum had promised her a party in the garden. There would be birthday cake and balloons and a funny clown. All her friends were coming to her party.

There was only one problem! Pansy's two front teeth were loose. They wobbled whenever she bit into anything. How was she going to enjoy her party food?

"Mum," she asked, for the hundredth time, "will my wobbly teeth come out before my birthday party?"

"They'll come out when they're ready," said Mum, smiling.

That night Pansy woke suddenly. The curtains were open and her bed was covered in silvery moonlight. But that wasn't all! Sitting on Pansy's pillow was … can you guess? A fairy! It's true! She was tiny, with pale yellow wings, a wand and a sparkly dress.

Pansy could hardly believe it. She stared at the fairy, and the fairy stared back at her. The fairy spoke first.

"Can you see me?" she asked.

"Yes," said Pansy.

"That's funny," said the little fairy. "Usually I'm invisible!"

"Are you the tooth fairy?" asked Pansy.

"Yes, I'm Bobo," said the fairy. "I need two tiny front teeth to replace the keys on my piano."

Pansy showed Bobo her two front teeth. They were very wobbly.

"I hope they come out before my birthday party," said Pansy.

"They'll come out when they are ready," said Bobo. "If they come out before your birthday, I'll play my piano at your party!"

The next day, Bobo peeped into the playroom and found Pansy standing on her head!

"What are you doing, Pansy?" she asked.

"If I stay like this all day," said Pansy, "my teeth might fall out."

23

At teatime Bobo watched from behind a bowl of fruit, as Pansy ate all her cheese on toast, including the crusts. But still her teeth didn't come out!

"Try brushing your teeth," Bobo whispered to her, before Pansy went to bed.

"Oh yes! That will do it!" said Pansy. And she brushed and brushed and brushed, but the wobbly teeth just stayed stubbornly in her mouth.

The day before Pansy's birthday her two front teeth came out! It didn't hurt one little bit.

"Look!" she said to Mum, pulling a face, and showing a big gap where her teeth should be.

"Scary! Scary!" laughed Mum, pretending to be frightened.

24

"These are for Bobo," said Pansy, showing Mum the teeth.

"Who's Bobo?" asked Mum.

"The tooth fairy, of course," said Pansy.

That night Pansy went to bed early. She put her teeth under the pillow.

"I'll just close my eyes for a minute," she said to herself, "but I won't go to sleep."

Later Bobo came in, but Pansy had already dozed off. Bobo even whispered Pansy's name, but Pansy was fast asleep.

Pansy didn't wake until the sun shone through her curtains the next morning. The first thing she did was look under the pillow.

25

The two tiny teeth had gone! In their place were two coins.

Pansy's fifth birthday party was the best she'd ever had. All her friends came. There was jelly and ice cream, balloons and the funniest clown she'd ever seen.

Her friends sang 'Happy Birthday' so loudly that Mum had to put her fingers in her ears. But only Pansy could hear the tiny fairy playing a piano and singing 'Happy Birthday' in a silvery voice.

26

The Flower Fairy

The fairies at Corner Cottage were always busy. The garden was full of flowers and it was the fairies' job to look after them. You never saw them because they worked at night and hid during the day.

Blossom, the youngest fairy, was also one of the busiest. It was her job to paint all the bluebells.

Corner Cottage had a lot of bluebells. They spread out under the apple tree like a deep blue carpet.

One evening, Blossom was sick.

"I've got a terrible cold," she told her friend Petal, sniffing loudly. "I don't think I can work tonight."

"I wish I could help," said Petal, "but I've got to spray the flowers with perfume or they won't smell right. You'll have to ask the gnomes."

Oh dear! Nobody liked asking Chip and Chuck, the garden gnomes. All they liked doing was fishing and windsurfing on the pond and playing tricks. Blossom was very worried about asking them.

"No problem!" said Chip and Chuck when she asked them. "Just leave it to us."

28

But Blossom was right to worry! When she got up the next morning the gnomes had painted some of the bluebells ... YELLOW! She couldn't believe it.

"Have you seen what they've done?" she said to Petal. "What will Jamie think?"

Jamie lived in Corner Cottage with his mum and dad, and he played in the garden every day. That morning he came out as usual and made for the apple tree. It was a great tree for climbing. As he sat on his favourite branch, he looked down. Something looked different.

"I'm sure those flowers were blue yesterday," he thought.

"Mum," he said, going into the kitchen, "I've picked you some flowers."

"Yellowbells?" said Mum, putting them into a jam jar.

29

"Where did you get these?"

"Under the apple tree," said Jamie.

"How odd," said Mum. "I don't remember planting those."

That night, Blossom was still feeling ill.

"You'll have to paint the yellowbells again," she told the gnomes. But Chip and Chuck just chuckled.

In the morning, Jamie ran out to the garden and climbed the apple tree. This time the flowers were pink! He picked a bunch for his mum and she put them in the jam jar with the yellowbells.

30

When Petal told Blossom what had happened, Blossom groaned.

"I just knew something like this would happen." But she was still feeling too sick to work.

"Don't worry," said Petal. "Leave it to me." Petal made the naughty gnomes paint all the pinkbells again.

And this time she watched them carefully. The naughty gnomes grumbled loudly.

"Do it," said Petal, "or you'll never fish or windsurf on the pond again!"

The next morning, all the bluebells were blue again. Blossom was feeling much better.

"I'll be glad to get back to work!" she told Petal.

When Jamie and his mum went into the garden, everything was as it should be. The bluebells were the right colour. And there was no sign of the yellowbells or pinkbells.

"It must have been the fairies!" joked Mum.

That night, as Jamie lay in bed he heard laughing and splashing from the fishpond. But, when Jamie peered through window, he couldn't see anything.

"Maybe it really was the fairies," he thought as he drifted off to sleep.